AR Quiz # 43127
BL: 4.2
AR Pts: 1.0

W9-BBQ-152

Sheltie

Saves the Day!

Written and illustrated by **Peter Clover**

ALADDIN PAPERBACKS

New York   London   Toronto   Sydney   Singapore

For Mum and Dad

First Aladdin Paperbacks edition May 2000

ALADDIN PAPERBACKS
An imprint of Simon & Schuster
Children's Publishing Division
1230 Avenue of the Americas
New York, NY 10020

Library of Congress Cataloging-in-Publication Data
Clover, Peter.
Sheltie saves the day! / written and illustrated by
Peter Clover. — 1st Aladdin Paperbacks ed.
p.   cm. — (Sheltie ; #2)
Summary: With the help of her clever Shetland pony, Emma tries to find a
way to keep her neighbor from selling her beloved Horseshoe Pond to
some unscrupulous buyers who want to turn it into a campground.
ISBN 0-689-83575-2 (pbk.)
[1. Ponies—Fiction. 2. Buried treasure—Fiction.] I. Title.
PZ7.C62475Sk   2000
[Fic]—dc21   99-87887

⭐ Chapter One

That morning, Emma's mom and dad had decided to paint the wooden gate at the front of the house. Mom was busy with the sandpaper, rubbing the wooden posts smooth. Dad was stirring the paint and keeping an eye on little Joshua at the same time. Joshua kept trying to dip his fingers into the creamy white goo.

All three suddenly looked up as Emma

came racing up the driveway on Sheltie, her little Shetland pony.

Dad smiled. "Here comes the Lone Ranger," he said. Mom laughed and Joshua jumped up and down, clapping his hands together. He nearly kicked over the can of paint.

Joshua always got excited when he saw Emma riding Sheltie. He thought Sheltie was a racehorse. And if Emma ever took Sheltie over a jump, Joshua's eyes would grow wide like saucers.

Emma and Sheltie came to a halt with a clatter of hooves on the gravel path. Mom jumped back, startled.

"Did you forget to put the brakes on, Emma?" said Mom.

Dad had never seen her in such a hurry

before. Emma's face was all red. She looked very angry and upset. She jumped out of the saddle and landed with a thud.

"What's wrong?" asked Dad.

"It's Horseshoe Pond, Dad. It's awful," said Emma.

"Horseshoe Pond isn't awful at all, Emma," said Mom. "It's beautiful."

"I know," said Emma. "Horseshoe Pond *is* beautiful. That's why it's awful what they're going to do to it."

"Who's *they*?" asked Mom. "And what are *they* going to do?"

Sheltie began to snort and blow. He shook his long, shaggy mane.

"Sheltie thinks it's awful, too," said Emma. "Men are coming to fill in Horseshoe Pond. They're going to pull down all the trees and flatten Prickly Forest to make a rotten campground! It's awful, Mom."

"There must be some confusion," said Dad. "Horseshoe Pond is on Mr. Brown's farm. Mr. Brown would never let a thing like that happen. A campground? I don't think so, Emma."

"But it's true, isn't it, Sheltie?" said Emma.

Sheltie scraped at the gravel with his hoof. He always did that when he was trying to tell Emma something.

"I overheard Mrs. Jenkins talking to the gardener. Mrs. Jenkins said it was the worst news she had ever heard. And that she'd gotten it straight from the horse's mouth. But I don't know which horse it was that told her."

Although it was a serious matter, Mom smiled and said, "That's only a saying, Emma. Horses don't really talk."

"Well, Sheltie does," said Emma. "I understand everything he says. Don't I, Sheltie?"

Sheltie's eyes twinkled beneath his long mane. He nodded his head three times.

"See?" Emma said brightly. "And Sheltie understands every word I say, too. Don't you, Sheltie?"

The pony nodded again.

Joshua gurgled and squealed with laughter.

"Anyway," said Emma. "Sheltie isn't a horse. He's a Shetland pony. A very special Shetland pony."

Emma threw her arms around Sheltie's neck and gave the little pony a big hug. Then she gave him one of his favorite peppermints. Sheltie loved peppermints.

Emma's dad went inside the cottage to telephone Mr. Brown. He was going to ask the farmer if Emma's story was true.

Five minutes later when Dad came out again, his face looked grim.

"It's true, I'm afraid," said Dad. "Every word of it."

Mr. Brown was in trouble. Last year his tractor broke down, and he was forced to borrow money to buy a new one.

This year he needed a new combine machine. Without it he wouldn't be able to harvest his cornfields in the autumn.

Mr. Brown needed money. And the only way he could get it was to sell off some of his land.

Two men were already interested in buying Horseshoe Pond and the big meadow. A little thicket of prickly holly brushes grew there, too, and it was all going to be taken away.

"I don't think there's anything anyone can do," said Dad. Emma lowered her

head and led Sheltie back to his paddock.
She felt very sad.

Chapter Two

Horseshoe Pond was one of Emma's favorite places. The pond was in the shape of a horseshoe, and where its two ends almost met and touched, there was a little hump of grass like an island. Emma liked to sit there and look out across the pond to the rolling hills, while Sheltie nibbled at the long grass.

There was a big sycamore tree that grew on the island. Emma would sit beneath it and listen to the birds as she watched the fish and the dragonflies.

Emma would pretend that she was a princess or a pirate queen and that the island was her castle or ship. And she'd imagine all the land as far as she could see belonged to her.

Emma couldn't imagine what Little Applewood would be like with no Horseshoe Pond and no magical island.

The next day, two men came in a jeep with shovels and spades. They put up a tent in Mr. Brown's meadow and set up camp.

When Emma and Sheltie came trotting along, the two men were already busy at

work. They were measuring things with a long tape and marking areas off all around the meadow with sticks and flags.

When the two men saw Emma and Sheltie, they both stopped and looked up. One of the men had black hair and a beard. The other man's hair was bright red and curly. Emma didn't like the look of them. Neither did Sheltie.

When Emma said, "Good morning," the two men just stared. The man with the beard spoke.

"And where do you think you're going, miss?"

"Horseshoe Pond," said Emma. "I always go there and sit under the tree."

"Well, not any more you don't," said the man. "You're not to come anywhere near here."

Sheltie gave a loud blow from his nostrils. Emma didn't like the way the man spoke. Then she heard a voice behind her.

"Emma can come here as often as she likes." It was Mr. Brown. He ruffled Sheltie's long mane as he spoke. "Don't you take any notice, Emma. The meadow hasn't been sold yet. It still belongs to me. I've only given these men permission to take measurements and make some tests before the sale goes through. In the meantime you can come here whenever you want."

Mr. Brown gave the two men a stern, no-nonsense look. They grumbled under their breath and stomped off over to their jeep.

Mr. Brown turned and spoke to Emma. His voice was kind and filled with sadness.

"You can sit by the pond as long as you wish, Emma," he said. "Those men won't bother you."

Emma gave a weak smile, then rode Sheltie over to the pond and jumped down from the saddle. Sheltie bent his head and nibbled on the fresh green shoots that grew there. Emma sat on the little island and watched Mr. Brown walk back to the farm.

Emma didn't want to stay there for long because the two men kept looking over at her. But she felt that she should sit there for a little while because Mr. Brown had been so kind.

Chapter Three

A few minutes later, the man with red hair came walking across the meadow. Emma's heart was beating fast.

"Hello," said the man. He sounded friendly. "I'm sorry if my friend was rude before, but we have a lot of work to do, and we can't get on with it if there are too many people around."

Emma didn't say anything. She wished Mr. Brown would come back. Sheltie stopped munching grass and looked up. His eyes shone, bright and alert. Emma noticed that the man was holding a piece of paper. The paper looked old and worn at the edges.

"What are you measuring?" asked Emma.

"Um, we're measuring for the drains," said the man very quickly.

"And do you really have to fill in the pond?" asked Emma.

"Of course," said the man. "We can get at least three RVs where that pond is."

Emma looked up through the leaves of the tree.

"Will you keep the tree?" asked Emma.

The man looked up at the big sycamore as though he had just seen it for the first time.

"It's only an old tree," said the man. He waved the piece of paper toward Prickly Forest. "All those will be coming down, too," he said.

Suddenly, without warning, Sheltie lurched forward and snatched the piece of

paper out of the man's hand. The man jumped, but Sheltie was very quick and ran off across the meadow with the piece of paper in his mouth.

The man was very angry and yelled at Sheltie as he galloped away. Emma leaped to her feet.

"Sheltie, come back!" called Emma. But Sheltie took no notice. He was off, running back to his paddock as fast as he could.

The other man saw what had happened. He dropped the spade he was holding and tried to cut Sheltie off at the gate. But Sheltie reached the gate first and charged along the road and up the driveway on his short little legs. The two men followed, huffing and puffing, with Emma running close behind.

When Sheltie reached the paddock, he flew into his little shelter at the end of the field. The two men were making a lot of noise. They were hollering and shouting so loudly that Dad came out of the house to see what all the fuss was about.

The two men were in the paddock, peering into Sheltie's field shelter. They were both shaking with rage as they watched a tiny corner of the paper disappear into Sheltie's mouth. With one gulp and a swallow it was gone.

"Oh, Sheltie. You naughty boy," said Emma. But deep down inside, Emma was pleased. She didn't like the two men one little bit.

"What is going on?" asked Dad. The man with the black beard pointed to

Sheltie. He jabbed at the air with his finger. "That *thing* has eaten our document!"

Dad asked the man to calm down and stop shouting. Mom had come out of the house now and came over to see what was going on. She held Emma's hand.

"He didn't mean to, honest," said Emma. "Sheltie's never done anything like that before. He's really sorry."

Just then, Officer Green, the village policeman, came riding up the lane on his bicycle. He heard all the shouting and rode straight into the paddock.

When the two men saw the policeman, they went very quiet.

"What seems to be the trouble?" said Officer Green.

Emma told the policeman what Sheltie had done. She said that Sheltie was very sorry.

The policeman said that under the circumstances there was nothing that could be done, and he sent the two men away.

Chapter Four

That evening, when Mom came upstairs to say goodnight to Emma, Emma was lying in bed looking up at the pictures on her bedroom wall. They were pictures of Horseshoe Pond and the big sycamore tree that grew there. Emma had drawn them herself.

"I think Sheltie knows that those men

are going to fill in the pond," said Emma. "That's why he ate their silly piece of paper."

Mom thought that perhaps Emma was right. She said goodnight and switched off the light.

All night long, Emma tossed and turned in her bed. She kept thinking of Horseshoe Pond and the new campground. She couldn't sleep a wink.

It was very late and dark when Emma heard Sheltie outside in his paddock. He was making funny whinnying noises. Emma got out of bed and looked out of the window.

In the moonlight she could see Sheltie standing by the fence. Emma looked beyond the paddock and out toward the meadow and Horseshoe Pond. In the daytime she could see the sycamore tree and just make out the water shimmering in the little pond. In the darkness Emma couldn't see a thing, but she looked all the same.

What is that? she thought. She looked hard. Emma could see a strange light moving around in the meadow. She stood at the window and watched the light in the meadow moving slowly to and fro.

Sheltie was still making funny noises and now he was pawing at the ground. Emma knew that Sheltie wanted to show her something. Emma decided to go and take a look. If she was quiet, then no one would ever know.

Emma got dressed and tiptoed downstairs. She unlocked the kitchen door and crept down the garden path. When Sheltie saw her, he gave a noisy blow and tossed his head.

"Shh, Sheltie!" Emma whispered as she unlocked the gate and went into the paddock.

Sheltie gave a little sneeze and urged Emma to follow him across to the far side of the field, where a tall hedge separated the paddock from Mr. Brown's meadow. The night was clear and warm. Emma looked up at the moon and stars twinkling in the sky. The moonlight made the hedge and all the grass shine like silver.

Emma climbed up on to the bank using the twisted roots like a ladder. She stood with one foot on Sheltie's back to steady herself.

"Stand still, Sheltie," said Emma. "And stop fidgeting!"

Emma peered over the top of the hedge into the meadow. She could clearly see that it was the two men walking about. One of the men was shining a flashlight on the ground. The other man was holding a funny kind of stick. On the end of the stick close to the ground was a flat, round disc.

It looked like a big frying pan with a very long handle.

The man was passing the frying pan slowly over the grass. A little light on the handle was flashing as he walked along. As Emma's eyes got used to the dark, she could see that the man with the frying pan was wearing headphones.

Every now and again the man stopped, and the other one marked the spot with a small yellow peg.

What are they doing? thought Emma. *And why are they doing it in the middle of the night?*

Whatever it was, she guessed it must be something secret. Something they didn't want Mr. Brown or anyone to know about.

✪ ✪ ✪

The next morning, Emma woke bright and early. She had a bowl of cereal for breakfast, then went outside to feed Sheltie. One scoop of pony mix plus one tiny handful for luck.

Normally, Sheltie would push his nose into the feeding manger before Emma had finished scooping. But today he just stood there and watched. He was blowing and snorting and stamping the ground.

"What is it, Sheltie?"

Emma was puzzled. Was he trying to tell her something?

Sheltie began scraping at the floor. As he pushed the hay aside, Emma noticed a piece of paper lying on the floor. It was the same paper that he had snatched from the two men the day before.

Sheltie hadn't eaten it after all! He had been pretending and had only bitten off and swallowed one tiny corner.

Emma picked up the paper and held it in both hands. It was a map. An old drawing of Little Applewood. She recognized the meadow from the horseshoe shape of the pond. The sycamore tree and the thicket of shrubs and bushes were clearly marked.

Emma found her house on the map and traced her finger along the road down to the meadow. The farm was also marked and so was Fox Hall Manor. There were also lots of crosses drawn all over the paper. Emma counted them. There were at least twenty.

Emma turned the map over. On the back of the paper, printed at the very top in fine, fancy letters was a name and address. *Major Armstrong, Fox Hall Manor, Little Applewood, Chittlewink*. The map scribbled on the back of old notepaper from the manor house.

Emma didn't know what to do. She thought it best to show Mom and Dad right away. But Dad had already gone off to work, and Mom was busy in the kitchen, making posters for the local police force's charity dinner.

Little Joshua sat at the table watching. Mom was trying to keep him out of the paint cans. His hands were already covered with sticky glue.

"Oh, Emma," said Mom. "Would you be an angel and take these muffins down the road to Mr. Crock? They're to say thank you for all those carrots he gave me the other day." Six muffins were packed into a little red tin on the table.

Emma put the map in the pocket of her jeans and took the muffins. She decided to show Mom the map later, when she wasn't so busy.

Chapter Five

Mr. Crock was in his vegetable garden planting turnips. Sheltie stuck his nose over the stone wall and whinnied. When Mr. Crock looked up and saw that it was Sheltie, he smiled.

"Hello, Emma," he said. They had become good friends, and Mr. Crock wasn't half as grumpy as he used to be. He thanked

Emma for the muffins and asked if she would like one with a glass of homemade lemonade.

Emma followed Mr. Crock into the kitchen and watched him pour two drinks from a big jug. Sheltie looked in through the kitchen window. Emma had made him promise to be on his best behavior.

As Emma ate her muffin and drank her lemonade, she decided to show Mr. Crock the map, and tell him all about the two men and their funny frying pan.

Mr. Crock listened carefully to every word. Then he held the map and studied both sides of the paper.

"I think I know just what this is, Emma," he said. "Many years ago, before the old Major died, he started to worry that robbers might steal his valuables. So one day, the silly old fool gathered together all his treasures and took them out and buried them! He buried his treasure in some secret place, then forgot where he'd buried it.

"His family was very upset and searched everywhere, because part of the treasure that Major Armstrong had buried was the family collection of gold coins.

"There was a story that he'd drawn a map, but he couldn't remember where he'd put that either. No one ever found the map and the treasure was lost. The Major must have hidden the map in an old book or something.

"You know what I think this is, Emma? Major Armstrong's lost treasure map."

"And those two men must have found it, and they're looking for the old Major's treasure!" said Emma.

Mr. Crock told Emma that the men's funny frying pan was probably a metal detector.

"People use them to find metal objects, such as coins, buried beneath the ground."

"What are we going to do?" asked Emma. "Should we tell the police?"

Mr. Crock thought hard for a moment. "Perhaps it would be best for now if we didn't tell anyone, Emma. After all, those men haven't really done anything wrong. And we can't prove that they are looking for Major Armstrong's treasure, can we?"

"But if they do find it, I bet they'll use the money to fill in Horseshoe Pond and

build their rotten campground," said Emma.

"Well, you'll just have to find it first," said Mr. Crock. "Why don't you take a walk up to Horseshoe Pond and see what those two men are up to?"

When they went back outside, Sheltie was standing with his head in an apple tree, helping himself.

"Sheltie, you naughty boy!" said Emma.

"It's all right, Emma," said Mr. Crock. "There are plenty of apples in that old tree. I don't suppose I'll miss one or two. But they're not very ripe yet. I hope Sheltie doesn't mind!"

Sheltie was full of mischief and pulled another apple from a branch of the tree.

"No, I don't think he minds at all," said Emma.

Chapter Six

Emma rode Sheltie back down the road to Mr. Brown's meadow. When they got to Horseshoe Pond there was no sign of the two men, but there were small holes dug all over the meadow next to the little yellow pegs.

Emma glanced at her wristwatch. It was ten o'clock.

"They must still be asleep in their tent, Sheltie," she said. "I expect they're very tired if they've been up all night digging these holes."

Sheltie looked at the holes and nodded. Then Emma had an idea.

"We'll come back nice and early tomorrow, Sheltie. And play a trick." Emma chuckled to herself as they walked away.

In the afternoon, Emma gave Sheltie's coat a good brush. As she untangled all the knots in his long mane, Emma thought about Major Armstrong and his treasure. *Imagine not remembering where he'd buried it all*, thought Emma. What a silly man he was!

Emma thought hard. She wondered where *she* would bury a secret treasure.

"I think I would bury it in a place where no one could see me digging," she told Sheltie. "Not out in an open meadow."

Sheltie cocked his head to one side. He was listening carefully to every word that Emma said. Emma began to comb Sheltie's long tail. It was so long it almost touched the ground.

"I would bury it somewhere hidden away. Somewhere where people would never go."

Then Emma thought of just the place. "I know, Sheltie!"

The little pony's ears pricked up.

"I would bury it under the biggest holly bush in Prickly Forest. No one would think of looking for it there."

Sheltie nodded and sneezed. He thought

Prickly Forest would be the perfect place, too.

The more that Emma thought about where she would bury the treasure, the more she wanted to go and take a look, just to see if old Major Armstrong himself had thought of that very same spot.

Emma decided to take Sheltie out for a ride. Prickly Forest seemed just the place.

Emma knew that the men would be working in the meadow. But she thought that if she kept to the far side of the field, she could sneak into Prickly Forest without being seen.

It was three o'clock when Emma rode Sheltie along by the back fence of the meadow. The two men were there, just as Emma expected. They were still poking around with sticks and digging little holes where the yellow pegs were.

Emma rode Sheltie over as close to Prickly Forest as she dared, then jumped down from the saddle and led the way into the bushes.

Sheltie stood on guard as Emma went to explore. But he quickly found a young shrub nearby with green, tender leaves and was soon munching his way through it.

Emma picked up a long stick. There were lots of small trees and shrubs growing there, as well as prickly holly bushes. Emma used the stick to brush the scratchy branches aside. There were stinging nettles too, so Emma had to be very careful. She made her way through the thicket to a big holly bush that she knew was there.

Emma stood before the big holly bush. It was covered with millions of prickly leaves and grew in a big round ball.

That's where I would bury the treasure! thought Emma. It would be very difficult for anyone trying to dig it up without getting scratched to pieces.

She walked around the bush, then crouched down on the grass and peered beneath the lowest branches. There was a small gap on one side, like a secret opening, which led into the middle of the giant bush. Emma crawled inside.

The prickly leaves pulled at her hair and caught on her sweatshirt. Emma pushed the branches aside with the stick. Then she prodded the stick ahead of her and poked at the ground.

The stick tapped against something solid. It was a rock—a large stone right in the center of the bush.

Emma inched her way forward. The rock was the size of a football, but flatter. A white cross was painted on top of the rock. The paint was gray and flaky in parts, but Emma could see the cross quite clearly.

Suddenly, a voice from behind her made Emma jump.

"What are you doing in there?"

Chapter Seven

Emma dropped the stick and crawled backward out of the bush. The man with red hair stood looking down at her with his hands resting on his hips. Emma looked up slowly. She felt her face turning crimson.

"Nothing!" said Emma. "I was just looking for mushrooms."

"Mushrooms don't grow under holly bushes!" said the man.

"Sometimes they do," said Emma. "They grow all over this forest."

"Well, you'd better look somewhere else. We don't like kids messing around when we're working, and we want to come up here in a minute." The man turned away and walked back to the jeep.

Emma rushed over to Sheltie and jumped into the saddle. In minutes, she was racing back down the lane to tell Mr. Crock all about her discovery.

The next day, Mr. Crock met Emma in the paddock bright and early. He carried a shovel and a large plastic garbage bag. Emma had just finished giving Sheltie his breakfast and was filling the water trough from the garden hose.

"Here are the things you wanted, Emma. I can't come with you. I'm too busy. But you be careful and don't go getting yourself into trouble!"

It was eight o'clock when Emma and Sheltie rode down the driveway and up the road towards the meadow.

When they arrived, the two men were nowhere to be seen. They were both fast asleep inside their tent, just as Emma had thought they would be.

"We must be very quiet, Sheltie," Emma whispered.

She tiptoed over to some freshly dug holes. Then she made some new ones nearby. Emma reached into the carrier bag and pulled out some old tin cans. She

dropped them into the holes, then shoveled the earth back in. Sheltie helped by pressing the soil down with his hooves.

"This will give that metal detector something to find," chuckled Emma.

They buried all the tin cans as quickly as they could. Emma wondered what the

men's faces would look like when they dug them up, thinking it was Major Armstrong's treasure.

They tiptoed past the tent again on the way to Prickly Forest. Emma could hear the two men snoring inside. They were still fast asleep.

Emma led Sheltie to the big holly bush

and showed him the opening in the side. Sheltie gave a loud snort and shook his mane.

"Now, make sure that you keep watch properly this time," said Emma. Then she crawled inside the bush and ran her hand over the smooth stone with its white cross painted on the surface.

"Looks like we may have found something here all right, Sheltie," said Emma.

Sheltie kept watch while Emma moved the stone and began digging.

Chapter Eight

Emma had only been digging for a little while when her trowel hit something solid with a dull *clunk*. She pushed away the earth and uncovered a large metal box. The box had two rusty handles on each side and a big lock at the front.

It was about the size of a small suitcase and very heavy. Emma was so excited.

"It's the treasure, Sheltie! We've found Major Armstrong's treasure!"

Sheltie tossed his head and gave a loud snort.

Emma tried to drag the box out of the hole but it wouldn't budge.

"Goodness knows what's in here, Sheltie. It weighs a ton."

Just then, Emma glanced behind her through a gap in the trees and bushes towards the meadow. She saw the two men coming out of the tent. They stood there, yawning and stretching their arms.

"Oh, Sheltie! The men have woken up," said Emma.

When Sheltie looked over, both men were rubbing their eyes. They were still very sleepy and hadn't noticed Emma and Sheltie.

"We'd better hide this box again before they see us," said Emma. She crawled back into the bush, then recovered the box with dirt and placed the stone back on top.

Sheltie stayed well out of sight until the treasure was buried again. Then, keeping very low, Emma led Sheltie through the bushes to the far side of Prickly Forest. They followed the fence which ran along the back of the meadow, out of sight and away. The two men didn't notice a thing.

Emma's heart was thumping as they squeezed through a gap in the fence and joined the track that led back to the driveway.

When they got to the paddock Sheltie snorted and gave a loud blow as if to say "That was a close one!"

Emma was so excited that she could hardly breathe. She looked down and saw that her clothes were covered in mud.

Mom came out of the kitchen and went down to the paddock with little Joshua bouncing along behind. When Joshua saw Emma's muddy jeans he clapped his hands together and laughed.

"What on earth have you been up to, Emma?" said Mom. "You're filthy."

Emma's sneakers were muddy, too, and she had dirt all over her face and hands.

"Picking mushrooms," Emma said quickly. She glanced at Sheltie. "We've been looking for mushrooms in Mr. Brown's back field."

Mom didn't notice that they didn't have one single mushroom between them.

"You didn't have much luck!" she said.

"No," said Emma. "Maybe we'll be luckier tomorrow."

Mom looked puzzled.

"What are you two up to?" she said.

"Nothing," said Emma. Then she jumped

back into the saddle and trotted out into the road. "I'm just running over to see Mr. Crock for a minute," Emma called over her shoulder. "I won't be long."

Mom watched them disappear up the road. Then she turned to Joshua.

"I'm sure those two are up to something!"

That night, when everyone was fast asleep, Emma got out of bed and stood by the window. She looked out into the darkness over to Horseshoe Pond.

Emma could see the lights moving about in the meadow again. She smiled to herself. She imagined the two men's faces as they dug up the old tin cans.

I bet they'll be really mad, she thought.

She could see Sheltie standing by the paddock fence and blew him a good-night kiss.

See you in the morning, Sheltie. Tomorrow is Treasure Day!

Chapter Nine

Emma was up and dressed by half past seven. She pulled on her riding boots and went downstairs.

"My goodness, Emma," said Dad. "You're up early."

Dad wasn't working today. He was going to start stripping the old wallpaper off Joshua's bedroom walls. Mom was already busy at the kitchen table finishing her posters for the charity dinner.

"Where are you off to then?" said Mom.

"Sheltie and I are taking Mr. Crock mushroom picking in Mr. Brown's back meadow," said Emma. "We have to be there early to pick the best ones."

"Well, we'll look forward to having mushrooms in our soup for lunch, won't we, Joshua?" said Dad. "That is, if Sheltie doesn't eat them all first."

Moments later, Mr. Crock arrived pushing a wheelbarrow. Sheltie stood with his ears pricked up and whinnied, shaking his head.

"Little devil," growled Mr. Crock.

"Morning, Mr. Crock," Mom said as

she wandered out into the yard. She smiled when she saw the wheelbarrow.

"Do you think you might fill the whole wheelbarrow? That would keep us all in mushrooms for years!"

"I thought I might as well collect some firewood while I'm at it," said Mr. Crock. "No sense in wasting a trip to the forest."

"Well, good luck," said Mom. She stood at the back door and watched as Emma and Sheltie led Mr. Crock and his wheelbarrow up the road.

It was still and almost quiet in Mr. Brown's meadow. The two men were snoring soundly inside their tent, fast asleep.

As they pushed the wheelbarrow past the tent, Emma noticed a heap of old tin cans piled up by a number of freshly dug holes. Emma and Mr. Crock looked at each other and exchanged a secret wink.

"I bet they were surprised when they dug those up!" whispered Emma.

They wheeled the barrow into Prickly Forest. Sheltie led the way and pushed aside all the prickly branches. His coat was very thick, so he didn't feel any of the scratchy twigs and leaves.

They parked the wheelbarrow next to the big holly bush. Inside the wheelbarrow was an old blanket. Mr. Crock took the blanket and laid it on the grass. Then Emma took the small shovel and crawled into the bush.

It was much easier this time. Emma pushed the stone aside and shoveled the

loose earth away. Mr. Crock kept watch through the trees, checking the tent across the other side of the handles. Then Sheltie dragged the metal box out on to the grass.

Emma shoveled all the earth back into the empty hole and replaced the rock. She stood there with Sheltie and Mr. Crock looking down at the treasure chest.

"Best not to try and open it here," said Mr. Crock. "Let's get it away safely and take it to Officer Green. He'll know what to do."

Mr. Crock helped Emma to lift the box. It was very heavy, but they managed to load it into the wheelbarrow. Then Emma covered the box with the blanket.

"There, that's done," said Mr. Crock. "Now all we have to do is get this wheelbarrow past that tent before those two sleepyheads wake up."

Emma felt her heart sink in her chest. Her legs suddenly felt all wobbly. As she glanced over into the meadow she saw the two men standing by the tent!

Chapter Ten

The two men were both looking over towards Prickly Forest.

"Oh, no!" said Emma. "They've seen us. They're coming over. What shall we do?"

Mr. Crock began to pick up odd bits of branches and old twigs.

"Hurry, Emma. Pile as much firewood

as you can into the wheelbarrow!"

They worked as fast as they could, covering the blanket and treasure chest with dry twigs. Soon the wheelbarrow was piled high.

The two men strode into the thicket. The treasure chest and blanket were hidden from view. Well, almost.

"What are you two doing snooping around?" said the man with the black beard. He looked very angry and carried a big stick in his hand.

"We're not snooping around," said Emma. "We're collecting firewood. Mr. Brown doesn't mind. It keeps the thicket clear and it's good wood for the burner."

"Collecting firewood in the middle of the summer. Sounds a bit funny to me."

"Not as funny as digging holes all over the meadow," growled Mr. Crock. "What are you two up to anyway?"

"None of your business," snapped the man. "Now take that pony and that rotten old wheelbarrow out of here and be on your way. We've got important work to do!"

Emma and Mr. Crock were only too happy to be on their way. Emma helped Mr. Crock lift the wheelbarrow handles and they started to push. But the barrow was very heavy and it took all of their strength to make it move.

"A bit heavy for a load of old twigs, isn't it?" said the man with the beard. "Just what else have you got in there?"

The man with the red hair glanced down at the wheelbarrow. He could see a corner of the blanket poking out at the side.

"What's this?" he said, reaching forward and grabbing the blanket. He gave it a hard tug and all the firewood fell onto the grass. They all stood there, staring down at Major Armstrong's treasure chest.

"Well, well, well. And what have we here?" said the man with the black beard. He tapped on the metal box with his stick. "Been doing a bit of digging on your own, have you?" he said. "Seems like you two have found exactly what we've been looking for! Get some rope from the jeep, Red."

Emma shouted. "Run, Sheltie! Run!"

The man swung the stick, but Sheltie was off, galloping away through the thicket.

"Hurry with that rope, Red. I'll keep these two here."

Emma felt like crying. Tears welled in her eyes but she was determined to be brave.

The man pointed the stick at Mr. Crock.

"Now you just behave yourself and keep quiet. And don't do anything stupid!"

Mr. Crock stood with his hands at his side. Emma's legs felt like jelly.

The other man came back with the rope and tied them up.

"Put them against that tree, Red," said the man waving the stick.

Emma and Mr. Crock sat beneath the tree with their hands and feet tied together.

"You won't get away with this," said Mr. Crock.

"I think we will," said the man. "It won't take us long to pack up our things and be on our way."

"But we'll tell the police," said Emma. "And you won't be able to use the treasure

to buy the meadow or build your rotten campground."

"We never planned to build a campground," said the man. "It was just an excuse to dig for the treasure. And now we've got what we came for, and nobody is going to stop us!"

"You can't leave us here," said Emma.

"I can do anything I want," laughed the man. "And it's no use calling for help either. Mr. Brown has gone out for the day, and the other houses are too far away for anyone to hear." The man gave a horrible, mocking laugh.

"Don't worry, Emma," said Mr. Crock. "Your mom will come looking for us when you don't turn up at the house for lunch."

"And we'll be long gone," laughed the two men. They each took a handle of the heavy metal box, and carried the treasure chest away. Emma and Mr. Crock watched as the two men hurried to pack up all their things.

"Oh dear," sighed Emma. "What are we going to do now?"

Then she had an idea. Sheltie. Of

course. He must be hiding somewhere. Sheltie would know what to do. She took in a deep breath and called out at the top of her voice:

"SHELTIE!"

Chapter Eleven

Sheltie wasn't very far away. He was in the next field behind a hedge. The little pony's ears pricked up as he heard Emma's voice.

Sheltie cocked his head to one side, listening. He trotted out into the middle of the road.

Something was wrong. Where was Emma?

Sheltie looked around. His nostrils flared as he sniffed at the air. Then he galloped over to the fence as fast as he could and stuck his head over the top rail.

Sheltie looked up and down the meadow. He couldn't see Emma anywhere, but he could see the two men. And they were coming out of Prickly Forest carrying the metal box.

"SHELTIE!" Emma called again.

This time Sheltie knew that Emma was in trouble and needed help.

Sheltie gave his head a good shake and blew a loud snort. Then, eyes bright and alert, he galloped down the road back to the house.

When he got there, the front gate was locked. The gate had been fitted with a

new safety bolt to keep Joshua from running out into the road.

Sheltie looked at the bolt. It was just like the special bolt on his paddock gate. Sheltie saw the little pin which held the bolt in place and carefully pulled it free with his teeth. Then he slipped the bolt across and pushed the gate with his nose. Sheltie trotted round to the back of the cottage.

Officer Green's bicycle was propped up against the cottage wall. He was inside collecting the posters Emma's mom had made.

Sheltie scraped at the kitchen door with his hoof. Emma's mom heard Sheltie outside and opened the door. Sheltie stamped his feet and pawed at the ground.

"What is it, Sheltie? What's the matter?" said Mom. It was almost as if Sheltie were trying to tell her something. She stood at the open door and looked past the pony down the garden and into the empty paddock.

"Where's Emma?" said Mom. "Is it Emma, Sheltie?"

Dad came out of the cottage with Officer Green.

"What's going on?" said the policeman.

"It's Sheltie," said Mom. "He wants to show us something. I think Emma's in trouble." She looked very worried. "Come on, Sheltie. Show us!"

Sheltie gave a loud snort and trotted off. He went a short way then stopped and looked back.

"We're coming," said the policeman.

Sheltie set off again looking back from time to time to make sure that Mom and the policeman were following. Dad had stayed behind to look after Joshua and watched from the front gate as Sheltie led the way.

Chapter Twelve

The two men had finished loading the jeep. Major Armstrong's treasure chest sat between them on the front seat, and the engine was running, ready for their get-away.

The jeep rolled forward just as Sheltie burst through the gate into the meadow.

Sheltie ran straight at the jeep at a flat-out gallop. The man with the black beard was driving.

Suddenly Sheltie stopped, right in front of the moving jeep. The brave little pony stood his ground as the jeep roared towards him.

Emma and Mr. Crock could see what was going on from Prickly Forest. Emma gasped as she realized that Sheltie wasn't going to move out of the way.

At the last moment the jeep swerved to go around Sheltie. The sudden turn made the front wheels stick in one of the freshly dug holes and the jeep's engine stalled. Emma breathed a sigh of relief.

Sheltie turned and kicked out with his strong back legs. He kicked as hard as he could. His hooves hit the side of the jeep with a loud thud and made two big dents in the driver's door.

The other door of the jeep flew open and the man with the red hair jumped out and tried to run away. Officer Green brought him down with a flying tackle and knocked the air right out of him. The man lay on the grass, unable to move.

Sheltie stood guard over him, stamping his hooves just in case he decided to run off again.

The driver had hit his head when the jeep stopped so suddenly. He sat forward in his seat, dizzy and dazed.

Officer Green pulled the door open and reached inside the jeep. He took the jeep's keys and handcuffed the man to the steering wheel.

"Over here! We're over here!" called Emma.

Officer Green called the station on his police radio while Mom ran over to the thicket. She found Emma and Mr. Crock tied up beneath the tree. She quickly undid the ropes.

"I knew Sheltie would bring help," said Emma. "I just knew it!" She blurted out the whole story to Mom.

"We found the treasure—Major Armstrong's treasure—and now we can save Horseshoe Pond!"

Mom gave Emma a big hug. She was so relieved to find that Emma was safe.

A police car pulled up alongside the meadow to take the two men to the police station. Emma ran up to Sheltie and threw her arms around his neck. Sheltie's eyes twinkled and he gave a loud snort.

"Oh, Sheltie, you're so clever," said Emma. Mr. Crock and Officer Green agreed.

"You always know just what to do!" said Emma.

Sheltie pawed at the ground with his hoof.

Back at the house, Officer Green opened the big metal chest. The lock was all rusty and the box had to be opened with one of Dad's drills and a pair of pliers. Inside the

box were Major Armstrong's treasures—
the valuables he had buried all those years
ago.

There were silver candlesticks, twelve
silver goblets, a set of silver spoons, two
little gold statues and all of Major
Armstrong's war medals. And in a big

black velvet bag was the family's collection of old gold coins.

"This lot must be worth a fortune," said the policeman. "The Armstrongs will be very pleased to hear about this!"

And indeed they were.

Up at Fox Hall Manor the family was delighted to hear of Emma's find. They offered a big reward.

As the treasure was found on Mr. Brown's land, Emma and Mr. Crock thought it was only right that the reward should go toward helping the farmer and saving Horseshoe Pond.

There was enough reward money to help Mr. Brown without him having to sell off one piece of land. Horseshoe Pond was going to stay exactly as it was. Little

Applewood would remain a peaceful little town, thanks to Emma and Sheltie!

That evening Emma went out to the paddock with a bagful of fresh carrots. Sheltie was frisky, tossing his head and swishing his tail. When he saw Emma with the carrots he ran over and snatched the whole bag out of her hands. Then he ran off around the paddock, carrots spilling everywhere.

Emma laughed. "Oh, Sheltie, you *are* naughty sometimes. But you're the best pony in the whole wide world!"

Sheltie munched the carrots and snorted. He had to agree. He *was* the smartest little pony ever.

Sheltie ACTIVITY FUN PAGES
Developed by Stasia Ward Kehoe

SHELTIE SAVES THE DAY! QUESTIONS

1. What is the name of the town in which Emma's family lives?
2. When Horseshoe Pond is filled in, what do the two strange men say they plan to put in its place?
3. What is special about the piece of paper Sheltie steals from the men?
4. Who is said to have buried treasure near Horseshoe Pond?
5. To whom do Emma and Mr. Crock think the treasure reward money should be given? (answers below)

GOOD LUCK HORSESHOE

Some people believe that hanging a horseshoe over your door brings good luck. To make your own lucky horseshoe, you will need some help from an adult and . . .

- A sheet of old newspaper
- A piece of light cardboard (such as one side of an empty cereal box)
- A pencil

1. Little Applewood 2. A campground 3. It is a treasure map. 4. Major Armstrong 5. Mr. Brown

- Safety scissors
- A handheld hole punch
- Paint
- Craft glue
- Beads, glitter, plastic buttons, ribbons and/or other craft materials

Cover your work surface with the newspaper. Lay the cardboard on the work surface. Use the pencil to draw a large horseshoe shape, like the one pictured above, on the cardboard. Cut out the horseshoe shape. Use the hole punch to make one hole at the top center of your horseshoe. Paint the horseshoe a cheerful color. When the paint is dry, glue on beads, glitter, or buttons. Or, attach some bright ribbons. Hang your lucky horseshoe over your bedroom door!

TERRIFIC TREASURE MAPS

Colonel Armstrong made a map to show the location of a hidden treasure. You can make your own treasure map. Fill a small plastic container with pennies or small toys. Hide your "treasure" in your backyard or your house. (Hint: Check with an adult to make sure your hiding place is permissible.) Draw a map leading from your front door to the "treasure." Mark the treasure spot on your map with an "X." Draw a line from the door to the treasure, or write a few good clues like: "Take five steps west from the mailbox" or "Turn left at the couch." Use a stopwatch to see how long it takes your friends to find the treasure. Or make several copies of your map and have a treasure hunt race.

SAVE THE DAY IN YOUR COMMUNITY

Emma and Sheltie help save Horseshoe Pond and keep Little Applewood beautiful. Ask a parent, teacher, or librarian about efforts to keep your community beautiful and join in. Or, team up with friends to plant flowers, pick up litter, promote recycling, or protect wildlife where you live.

FAMOUS HORSES FROM HISTORY

Horses have stamped their hoofprints on history and literature from Ancient Greece to modern America. Can you match the names of these historic horses to their famous human friends? Write your answers on a separate piece of paper, and then check them against the answers below. Go to your local library or do some online research to learn more about these historic horses.

1. Marengo
2. Copenhagen
3. Sultan (or Ivan)
4. Nelson
5. Flicka
6. Misty
7. Black Beauty
8. Black Stallion

(answers below)

A. Anna Sewell, author
B. Walter Farley, author
C. Duke of Wellington, English noble and military man
D. Mary O'Hara, author
E. Napoleon, emperor and military man
F. Marguerite Henry, author
G. George Washington, General and President
H. William "Buffalo Bill" Cody

PONY POINTERS: PREHISTORIC HORSES

Like Colonel Armstrong's gold, horses have a rich history. Scientists believe horses appeared on Earth about sixty million years ago—long before people. The earliest horse ancestor was a small, dog-like creature called Eohippus (EE-oh-hip-us) that lived in the Eocene period. Next came Mesohippus (MEZ-oh-hip-us), who lived about thirty-five million years ago and looked a lot like a small version of today's horses. Many fossils of Mesohippus have been found, especially in South Dakota. Merychippus (MARE-ee-kip-us) appeared

Answers: 7A; 8B; 2C; 5B; 1E; 6F; 4G; 3H

93

around the middle of the Miocene period. Merychippus had strong teeth for grazing and grew to the size of a modern pony. In the Pliocene epoch, Pliohippus (PLY-oh-hip-us), the direct descendent of today's horse, Equus (EK-wuhs), appeared. Like modern horses, Pliohippus had just one hoofed toe.